# MEL'S DINER

## MARISSA MOSS

Troll Medallion

For Simon and Elias
and with thanks to Shaletha Page

Copyright © 1994 by Marissa Moss.

Published by Troll Medallion, an imprint and trademark of Troll
Communications L.L.C.

First published in hardcover by BridgeWater Books.

Printed in the United States of America.

10  9  8  7  6  5  4  3  2  1

Library of Congress Cataloging-in-Publication Data
Moss, Marissa.
        Mel's Diner / by Marissa Moss.
            p.        cm.
        Summary: Mabel enjoys helping her father and mother run their
diner, a friendly and comfortable place where she loves to spend
time.
        ISBN 0-8167-3460-7 (lib. bdg.)    ISBN 0-8167-3461-5 (pbk.)
        [1. Diners (Restaurants)—Fiction.]    I. Title.
        PZ7.M8535Me    1994
        [E]—dc20                                        93-38683

It's morning at Mel's Diner. Coffee is brewing, bacon is sizzling, and biscuits are baking. They're the most wonderful smells in the world, and I smell them every morning.

My name is Mabel, and my family owns Mel's Diner.  None of us is named Mel.  He's the man we bought the diner from. We just kept the name because we liked it.

Every morning I help Mama and Pop with breakfast at the diner.  I set silverware on the tables so they're ready for customers, and I help make coffee.  Pop says when I'm bigger, I can make pancakes, too.

Mrs. Krupnick comes in first thing.

"Good morning, Mrs. Krupnick," I say.

"Good morning, dear," she says. "Coffee and a sticky bun, please." She always asks for coffee and a sticky bun. Sometimes I bring them to her before she even opens her mouth to ask.

Lila and Jorge come in next with the morning paper.  They sit in a booth, drinking cup after cup of coffee and reading the paper.  Sometimes they read me the funnies.

More and more people come in.  I bring them menus, serve food, and fill sugar bowls and napkin holders.  I keep the little glass by the cash register full of toothpicks.  There's always lots to do in our diner.

Sometimes I find treasures. I've found buttons and pens that people left behind. Once I found a pocketknife. Another time I found a ring. But because a woman came back the next day for the ring, I couldn't keep it. She was so happy I'd found it, though, she gave me a reward. That was an even better treasure!

Sometimes I sit and talk to people, like Mrs. Krupnick.
She tells me stories about when she was a little girl. I love to
hear the story of how it was so cold in the winter, the nearby
lake froze over. One January, her father made skates by tying
scraps of tin onto her boots. She tried to skate, but her feet
got so wobbly, she skated all the way across the ice on her
behind!

Other people, like Cole and Craig, tease me and tell me jokes.

"Knock, knock," says Cole.

"Who's there?" I say.

"Slater," says Craig.

"Slater, who?" I ask.

"Slater than you think!" they roar.

"You're right!" I say. "It *is* later than I thought. I've got to get to school."

They wave me out the door, still laughing at their joke.

After school, I do my homework with my best friend, Rhonda. We eat a big plate of French fries together. Rhonda loves the diner as much as I do.

Rhonda and I put money in the jukebox and dance together. We try out new steps. When we're finished, everybody claps. Somebody always offers another quarter so we can dance again.

When we get big, Rhonda and I are going to open our own diner.  We draw pictures of how it will look.  We think up names.  I like "Deedle Doodle Diner," but Rhonda likes "Eat Your Dinner Diner."

Lots of nights, Rhonda stays for dinner.  We have Jell-O for dessert because it's fun to wiggle it with our spoons.

"Stop wiggling that poor Jell-O and just eat it!" Mama says.

Rhonda and I giggle and wiggle.  Mama always says that, and we always keep on wiggling. That's the best part about Jell-O.

After Rhonda goes home, I help put away dishes and wipe the counter clean. Mama and I go home, but Pop stays at the diner late. He says he likes the quiet nighttime. I know what he means. The diner feels so bright and cozy in the dark night.

I look up at the stars and breathe the night air. It tastes cooler and fresher than daytime air, and I fill my lungs with it. I watch as the diner gets farther away, smaller and smaller, a spot of warm light in the darkness. Then we turn a corner and I can't see it anymore…

...but in front of us is another warm light—the light in our front window, welcoming us home.